For Rebecca

Published in the United States of America by Star Bright Books, Inc., New York. The name Star Bright Books and the Star Bright Books logo are registered trademarks of Star Bright Books, Inc. Please visit www.starbrightbooks.com.

Hardback ISBN-13: 978-1-59572-043-6   ISBN-10: 1-59572-043-X
Paperback ISBN-13: 978-1-59572-050-4   ISBN-10: 1-59572-050-2

Previously published under ISBN 0-19-279-676-3

Printed in China (WKT) 9 8 7 6 5 4 3 2

Library of Congress Cataloging-in-Publication Data

Wildsmith, Brian.
  The Owl and the Woodpecker / by Brian Wildsmith.
     p. cm.
  Summary: The owl and the woodpecker are anything but friendly neighbors until the day a storm hits their forest.
  ISBN-13: 978-1-59572-043-6 (hardcover)
  ISBN-10: 1-59572-043-X (hardcover)
  ISBN-13: 978-1-59572-050-4 (pbk.)
  ISBN-10: 1-59572-050-2 (pbk.)
 [1. Owls--Fiction. 2. Woodpeckers--Fiction. 3. Neighborliness--Fiction. 4. Forest animals--Fiction.] I. Title.

PZ7.W647Ow 2006
[E]--dc22
                                              2006004288

The Owl and the Woodpecker

Brian Wildsmith

Star Bright Books
New York

Once upon a time,
in a forest far away,
there lived a Woodpecker.

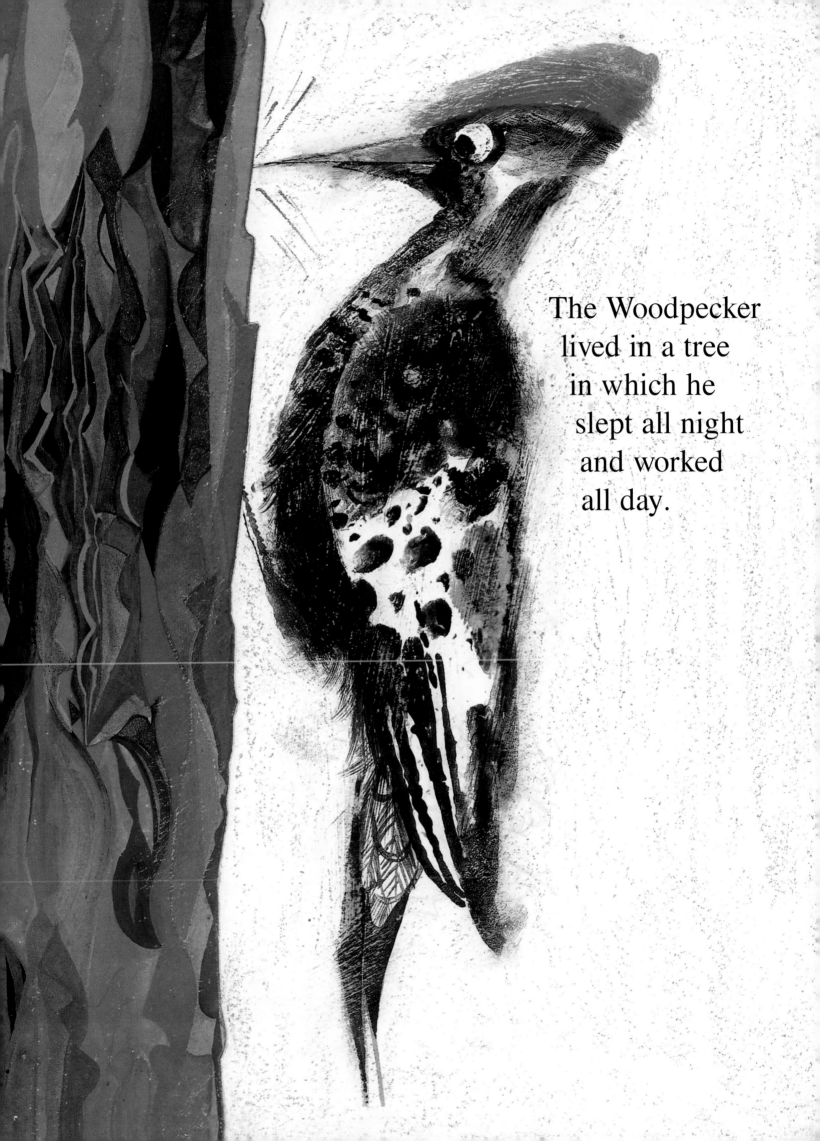

The Woodpecker
lived in a tree
in which he
slept all night
and worked
all day.

One day, an Owl
moved into the tree
next door. He liked
to work all night
and sleep all day.

Woodpecker pecked *so* hard and made *so* much noise that he woke Owl.

"Hey, you!" screeched Owl. **"How can I sleep with all that noise going on?"**

"This is my tree," Woodpecker said, *"and I can peck it as much as I want."*

Owl got *very* angry. His screeches and
hoots echoed through the forest. All the animals for miles
around came running to see what was the matter.

*"You carry on pecking,
Mister Woodpecker,"*
squeaked the mouse.

*"Owl is always
bossing and
chasing us around."*

"Oh, be quiet," growled the bear.

"Woodpecker, stop pecking, and let Owl sleep. We like a peaceful life around here."

Owl became *more* angry. He swooped down on the small animals, who quickly ran away.

They hid in all kinds of curious places.

"*You are a* BULLY!"

they shouted at him— when they were sure they were safe.

"What can I do to stop the noise?" Owl asked the big animals.

"We don't know," they said. "You are the wise and clever one. Perhaps you could move to another tree."

"*WHY SHOULD I?*"
snapped the Owl.
"*I like living in this tree.
That noisy Woodpecker
must move.*

But Woodpecker would not move. Day after day, his noisy pecking kept Owl awake.

And day after day, Owl became more and more tired and more and more bad-tempered. He began to be *so* grumpy and *so* rude that the forest animals decided they had to do something about it.

So they called a meeting.

"Something must be done," said the Badger.
 *"Woodpecker was here first,
 so Owl must leave."*

"But he says he will not leave his tree," replied Deer.

*"We can push down the tree,
and then he will have to leave,"*
said the crafty Fox.

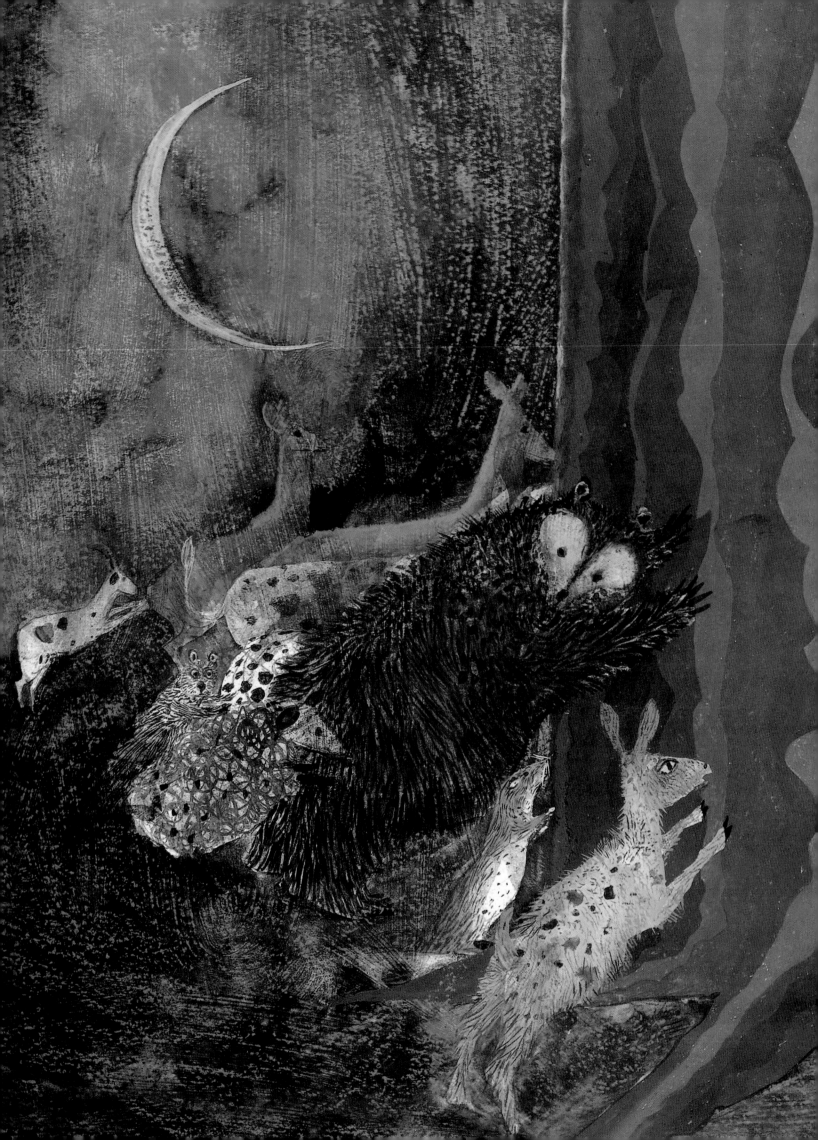

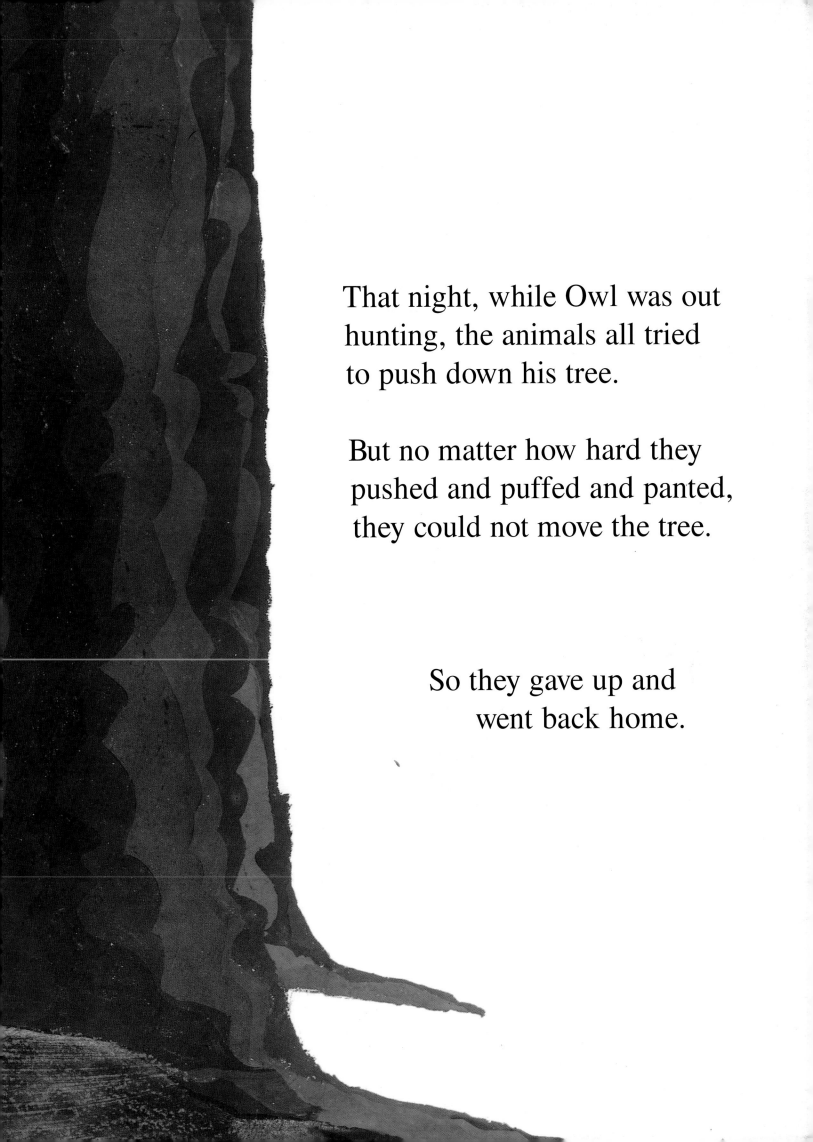

That night, while Owl was out
hunting, the animals all tried
to push down his tree.

But no matter how hard they
pushed and puffed and panted,
they could not move the tree.

So they gave up and
went back home.

Some time later, two
new animals came to the
forest. They were a pair
of beavers. They liked
Owl's tree, and started
to gnaw at the trunk.

Every day the beavers gnawed a little more.
It seemed as if they would gnaw right through the trunk!

One day,
a great storm
shook the forest.
The wind roared so
hard that Woodpecker
gave up his pecking.
    At last, Owl
    slept in peace.

Then Owl's tree
began to *creak*
and
   crack
and
g-r-o-a-n.

The wind grew
fiercer, but
Owl slept
soundly.
Then Owl's
tree began
to sway.

Woodpecker quickly struggled through the storm to Owl's tree. He pecked very loudly in Owl's ear.

Owl woke up. He was *very* angry, but then he realized why Woodpecker was pecking on his tree. Together, they flew to safety just as the tree crashed to the ground.

When the storm was over,
Owl thanked Woodpecker
for saving his life.

He was glad that Woodpecker
had been his neighbor.

So Owl and Woodpecker became good friends.
Woodpecker helped Owl find a tree in a quiet part
of the forest, where he could sleep all day without
hearing Woodpecker's noisy pecking.

Peace and quiet returned to the forest
and Owl and Woodpecker remained
good friends for the rest of their lives.